For my New York girlfriends...

and, of course, Jimmy!

For ordering information, write or telephone:

BARNABY & COMPANY PUBLISHING AND PRODUCTIONS, L.L.C.
P.O. Box 3198
Nantucket, MA 02584
Tel: 508.228.5114
888-5-BARNABY
E-mail: barnaby@nantucket.net

ISBN 0-9642836-9-7
Library of Congress Catalog Card Number: 99-96517

Summary: While Barnaby and his friends enjoy the seasonal activities in
New York's Central Park, they encounter challenges that reveal
the importance of cooperation and friendship.

BARNABY BOOK #5

Visit Barnaby's Web Site!

www.barnabybear.com

On a faraway land many miles out to sea,
There lives a young bear named Barnaby.
He is cute and adorable and cuddly, too,
He may be a bear, but he is just like you.

You may have heard! You may already know,
Because he makes new friends wherever he goes.
His red overalls and cap are all that he wears,
As he travels the world dashing here and then there.

Now he's off to New York to explore and explore.
He will stay with his aunt on the seventeenth floor.
Each season will be filled with fun trips to the park.
He'll have plenty to do there before it grows dark.

Walk, stroll, bounce, or run,
Hop on board, we'll have fun!
So, turn the page. Let the adventure begin!
You'll want to go with him again and again.

SUMMER SAILING

BAISLEY, BARNABY, MADISON, BAXTER, AND BORIS

EATING ICE CREAM
AFTER THE SUMMER SAILING FESTIVAL

It was a hot, humid day when Barnaby and his friends gathered for the Summer Sailing Festival in the park. They were excited, but also a little concerned. Last year Boris, the boar, had sunk all their sailboats with his huge submarine.

"This year my boat, the *Buoyant*, is unsinkable," Barnaby explained to his friends. "It's very strong and sturdy."

"Well, that bully Boris will not be able to catch my boat," boasted Madison. "It's an exact replica of a twelve-meter racing boat."

"Mine is so pretty that no one would ever want to sink it," said Baisley. "I've decorated it with the most colorful pansies and daisies."

"My boat looks very scary," added Baxter. "It's a pirate ship, and it is filled with tasty treasures...DOG BONES!"

Barnaby and his friends launched their boats into the little boat pond. Their sailboats gently drifted back and forth.

"Oh, no!" gasped Barnaby suddenly. "There's Boris again, with a *big battleship!*"

Moments later, the big battleship broadsided Baxter's boat.
"All my precious dog bones," whimpered Baxter.
"And my beautiful flowers," cried Baisley, as a giant wave from the passing battleship splashed over her boat's bow.
A flurry of flowers flew into the air.

"Boris, you don't make friends by sinking boats," shouted Barnaby across the pond.
Boris chuckled mischievously.

Madison quickly tightened the sails using his remote control.
"That pesky battleship will never catch my boat," said Madison.
But to his surprise, a puff of wind bent his fragile mast in half, and the flimsy
sail flopped sideways into the water.

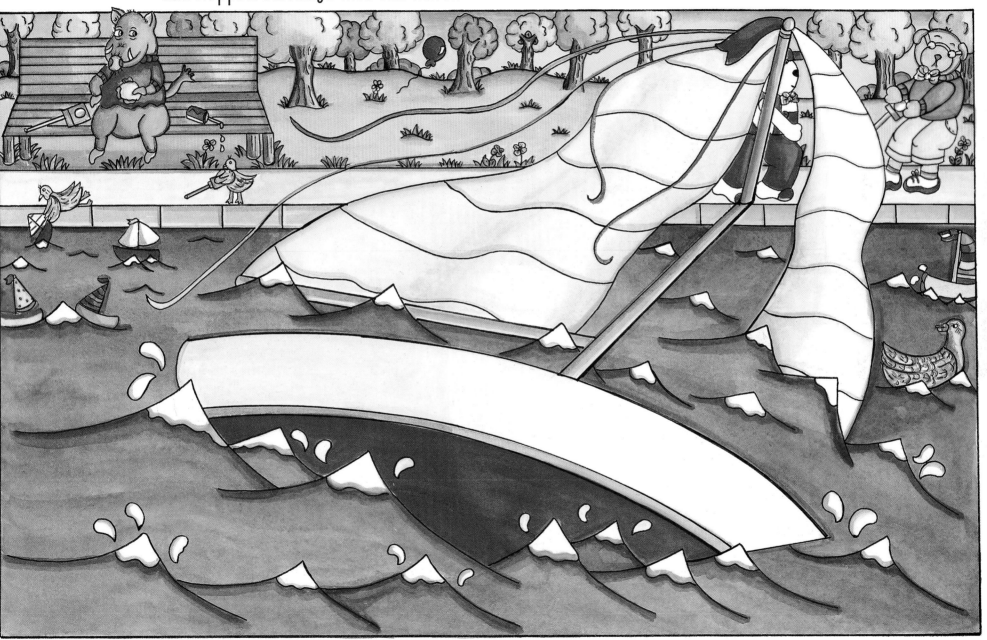

Boris sat all alone on the bench eating a bologna sandwich, smirking between bites.

Barnaby and his friends raced along the edge of the pond.

"Phew, the *Buoyant's* still safe," exclaimed Barnaby.

"Not for long," groaned Baxter.

Boris spun his battleship around and fired a volley of mud patties over, behind, and in front of the *Buoyant.*

Barnaby jumped into the pond to try to stop the battleship.

Baisley, Baxter, and Madison jumped in to help, too!

Soon, they were having such a good time laughing and splashing that they forgot all about the boats.
"This is just as much fun as sailing," shouted Barnaby.

Boris stood on the edge of the pond watching the others have fun. He suddenly felt very lonely.
"Maybe I shouldn't have been such a big, beastly bore!" he admitted to himself.

"Hey, Boris," shouted Barnaby. "Come on in!"
Boris was so excited to be included, for once, that he snorted gleefully and shook wildly.
He took a running leap and with one gigantic splash he even sank his own battleship!

FALL RELAY

BAXTER, JIMMY, BARNABY, BAISLEY, AND CECILE

BEFORE THE RELAY RACE IN CENTRAL PARK

At last the day had arrived for the Annual Fall Relay Race. Barnaby was very excited. He and his team had been practicing for months.

"Now," said Barnaby, gathering his teammates, "we must work together."

He looked over at the Fast 5th Avenue Five, who were stretching in unison.

In front was their famous captain.

"They call him Fast-Footed Farley," said Barnaby.

Fast-Footed Farley strutted over to Barnaby's team.
"I'm the fastest runner in this league," he bragged. "My team has won this
race for the past four years, and we're going to win again!"

As he turned to leave, he glanced back and shouted, "And by the way, your puny
seagull doesn't stand a chance against our fierce falcon."
Cecile, the seagull, trembled.
"Don't worry," said Baisley.
"Yeah, who does he think he is?" said Jimmy, the giraffe.
"We'll get out there and we'll do our best!" encouraged Barnaby.

The referee blew his whistle.
"Birds line up here, canines there, exotic animals here, and bears here and there,"
he instructed. "Now, everyone take your places."

Fiona, the fierce falcon, lined up next to Cecile. She sneered, sharpening her
talons, and moved even closer.
Cecile panicked.

"ON YOUR MARK! GET SET!"
The whistle blew, and the runners were off! Except for Cecile. She was hiding among a flock of pigeons.

Cecile was behind when she finally passed the baton off to Baxter.

"OH, NO!" moaned Baxter. "Heartbreak Hill! I'll never make it."
Suddenly, the sweet aroma of grilled sausages drifted down from Heartbreak
Hill. Baxter's pace quickened, and in a flash he was at the top.
"I'll have two hot dogs and a kielbasa to go," he drooled.

Baxter quickly licked the mustard off his jowls.
"Get ready, Jimmy," he shouted from afar.

Jimmy was so busy flexing his big, strong muscles that he didn't even hear Baxter coming.
"Hurry up," urged Baxter. "You have to catch that cheetah."

Jimmy was supposed to pass the baton to Baisley, but she had disappeared.
Moments later, she sprinted toward him with a handful of shopping bags.
"I'd been waiting for such a long time, and being so close to Fifth Avenue, well, I just
had to do a little shopping," she explained as she exchanged the bags for the baton.

Meanwhile, Gloria, the grizzly, gloated as she sauntered ahead.

Baisley ran, passing the baton to Barnaby.

"How did we get so far behind?" asked Barnaby.

"Ahh...we were a little distracted," admitted Baisley.

"Well, the race is not over yet," said Barnaby as he ran off to try to catch Fast-Footed Farley.

Barnaby rounded the corner and caught a glimpse of Fast-Footed Farley, who was casually strolling toward the finish line.

Barnaby's teammates crowded together.
"GO BARNABY GO!" they shouted.
Their cheers encouraged Barnaby to sprint fast and then faster.

At the last instant, Barnaby breezed by Farley, who was left flat-footed at the finish line.
"Hip, hip, hooray!" cheered Barnaby's friends. "Barnaby saved the day!"

WINTER LESSON

BARNABY, BAXTER, AND FRIENDS

AFTER A LONG DAY OF ICE SKATING

"Wake up, wake up, Baxter," nudged Barnaby. "It's a great day to go ice skating!"
Baxter peeked out from under his blanket, shivering as he glanced out the window at the snow-covered park below. Then he stretched one paw, feeling the cold wooden floor. Baxter was always making up excuses about why he couldn't go ice skating. "It's too cold," he would say, or "The ice skates will cramp my paws."
The truth is that Baxter had never been ice skating before, and the thought of falling all day on cold, hard ice was not his idea of fun.

But today, Baxter didn't have time to think of a new excuse. Barnaby had already pulled him out of bed...

dragged him down the hall...

and lured him into the park.

Baxter mumbled and grumbled as he followed Barnaby down the path to Wollman Rink.

Barnaby quickly put on his ice skates, jumped onto the ice, and did a slick hockey stop. Ice crystals sprayed into the air. Baxter just sat on the bench. "You'll never get me to ice skate," he muttered to himself.

Then Barnaby skated slowly by, holding a big juicy Park Burger. Baxter edged a little closer to the ice.

SNIFF, SNIFF. "Oh, okay, I'll give it a try," he agreed grudgingly.

Suddenly, his legs split in opposite directions. Then his feet slid from beneath him, and Baxter, Barnaby, and the Park Burger all landed on the ice.

"You see, falling is not so bad," encouraged Barnaby. "Let's try again!"

"Now, first, you must keep your hands out to the side and slightly in front of you for balance.
Stand tall, head up, and place your skates in a 'V' position. Now take a few short steps."
"It's called the duck walk," shouted a mother duck. "Quack, quack," chimed her ducklings.

Barnaby taught Baxter how to skate forward, backward, and then how to stop.

Baxter practiced all day. He was having so much fun that he didn't mind falling or looking goofy. By the afternoon he had really improved.

He even joined in as Barnaby led a train of skaters around the rink.

"Now, try this!" exclaimed Barnaby.
As a finale, Barnaby and Baxter lifted Polly and
Pammy, the poodle sisters, high above their heads.

However, Pammy's landing was not as smooth as she had hoped.

"Next winter we'll try skiing!" Barnaby suggested as they walked up the path.
"That's going to take more than *one* Park Burger," joked Baxter.

SPRING APPETITES

BARNABY AND ELLERY

OUTSIDE TAVERN ON THE GREEN

Early one morning, Barnaby was riding his bicycle around the park.

He zigzagged down the winding path and whizzed by the flowering cherry blossoms, smelling the sweet spring air.

"Hello, Barnaby!"
shouted the truly amazing juggler.

"Good morning, Barnaby!"
bellowed the gentleman who sells balloons.

"Bonjour, Monsieur Barnaby!" saluted the artist.

Suddenly, Barnaby screeched to a stop. Alongside the path was his good friend Ellery, the elephant, who was roller-dancing.

"Boogie-Oogie-Oogie," sang Ellery as he pranced and danced.

"Hey, Barnaby!" he shouted over the blaring music. "Let's Disco!"

Barnaby's feet twisted and his legs spun as he moved into the groove.

Together, Barnaby and Ellery boogied to the beat of "Disco 'Til You Drop."

"Let's hit it," said Barnaby. "I'm starved."

Barnaby and Ellery rode all around Central Park until they reached Tavern on the Green.

Barnaby walked inside the restaurant, and when he looked back, he didn't see Ellery.
"I'm stuck! I'm stuck!" whimpered Ellery.

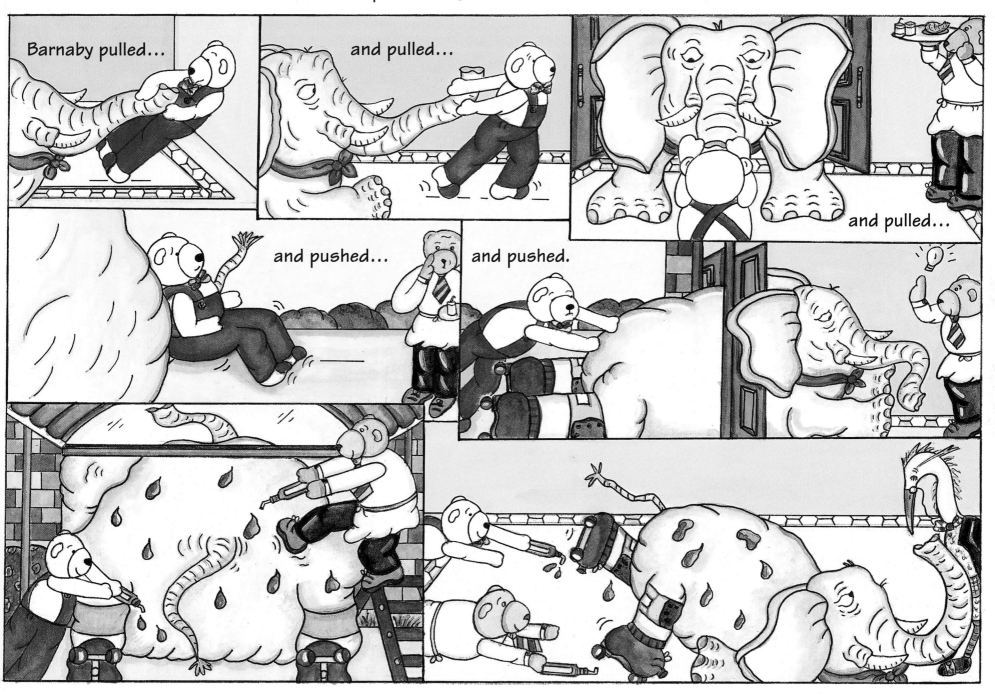

Then, with the help of a very nice waiter and a lot of olive oil...
Ellery came loose and all three of them came crashing into the restaurant.

NO!
ROLLERSKATES
TANK TOPS
CHILDREN
WITHOUT THE
SUPERVISION
OF AN
ADULT

"AHEM," coughed the Maitre d' as he cleared his throat. "May I help you, gentlemen?"

"We would like a table for two, please," requested Barnaby.

"I'm afraid we are completely booked. Yes indeed, we are completely full for lunch today. Do try again some other time. So sorry. Good day."

Barnaby turned to leave, but Ellery barreled through, spinning Barnaby toward the nearest open table. "BUT, BUT..." blurted the Maitre d'.

"I'll have the Beluga Caviar," said Ellery to the waiter. "It's the most expensive item on the menu," he whispered to Barnaby. "It must be huge."

The food arrived. Ellery's eyebrows rose, and the thick gray wrinkles on his face scrunched.
"What is this?" exclaimed Ellery.
"It looks like fish eggs," chuckled Barnaby.
"AHH! YUCK! BLAH! DISGUSTING!"

Then, out of the corner of his eye, Ellery spotted the dessert tray.
"Humm...yumm...double peanut butter chocolate chip pie! And peanut toffee hot fudge sundae!"

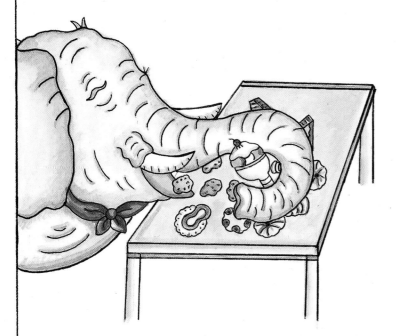

Ellery couldn't resist. With one swoop of his trunk, all the desserts disappeared!

The waiter immediately brought the check.
"$200!" gasped Barnaby. "You must have made a mistake! I only have $20!"
Barnaby looked over at Ellery, who simply shrugged his shoulders.

"YOU TWO! INTO THE KITCHEN, NOW!" ordered the waiter.
"This is so embarrassing," blushed Barnaby.
The Maitre d' poked and prodded Ellery toward a huge stack
of dirty dishes.

"What could be better than this?" Ellery mumbled happily, as he
inhaled another tasty chocolate morsel from the waiter's tray.